The Artist As A Young Girl

LIANA BROOKS

OTHER WORKS

HEROES AND VILLAINS

Even Villains Fall In Love
Even Villains Go To The Movies
Even Villains Have Interns
Even Villains Play The Hero (books 1 – 3 omnibus)
The Polar Terror

FLEET OF MALIK

Bodies In Motion
Change of Momentum
For Every Action (forthcoming)

ALL I WANT FOR CHRISTMAS

All I Want For Christmas Is A Werewolf
All I Want For Christmas Is A Reaper

SHORTER WORKS

Fey Lights
Prime Sensations
Darkness and Good

Find other works by the author at
www.lianabrooks.com

The Artist As A Young Girl

INKLET #43

LIANA BROOKS

Inkprint PRESS

www.inkprintpress.com

Print ISBN: 978-1-925825-42-8
eBook ISBN: 9781393670834

www.inkprintpress.com

National Library of Australia Cataloguing-in-Publication Data
Brooks, Liana 1982 –
The Artist As A Young Girl
36 p.
ISBN: 978-1-925825-42-8
Inkprint Press, Canberra, Australia
1. Fiction—Fantasy—General 2. Fiction—Short Stories

First Print Edition: October 2020
Cover image: 'The Turtle Dove' by Sophie Gengembre Anderson
Cover design © Inkprint Press
Interior art © Amy Laurens

THE ARTIST AS A YOUNG GIRL

Mother never liked the museum.

I didn't ask why when I was younger, only accepted it the same way I accepted my gray eyes, tumbling blonde hair, and my mother's refusal to let me wear purple. She hated the color.

I never asked why.

Piper, my brother, joined the family a few years after me. I don't remember him ever being a baby, but I was adopted.

At the very ancient age of seven, I knew all about how children came into the world.

Sometimes children were created, my mother said, and then abandoned. Left all alone. Hanging around, forgotten by the world.

My mother said that when she first saw me, she had to take me home. She knew it the same way she knew how to breathe. She knew it the same way I knew she was my mother.

She indulged my every whim.

Almost.

At seven I didn't notice. At twelve I barely thought to question the matter.

At fourteen I was properly infuriated.

I wanted to take an art class and Mother forbade me. That was the word she used. She stood in front of me and my best friend Liza and the guidance counselor and said, "I forbid you to take art class!"

I very nearly cried that night.

But Liza texted me and promised that she would take art class for the both of us while I joined choir. We had math and language together, so there was a perfectly good reason for us to meet a few hours after school each day and trade information.

It seemed like a glorious plan. Wondrous and freeing.

Mother was very pleased I wanted to join the choir. She said I sang like a dove. It was our little joke because my name is Sophie Dove Amberg.

After school each day, I went to Liza's house and drew and painted to my heart's delight. It made returning home each day so bleak.

There was no art in the house. Mother said it didn't go with the decor.

White. Black. Gray. That was the palette of home.

The only bright spots were Piper's toys scattered across the snow white carpet. His red fire engine the bright spot on a blank canvas.

That fire engine was still in the living room collecting dust the day I finally defied Mother.

Piper was playing music—instruments were his favorite toy—and I'd just gotten my driver's license.

"You should take your brother somewhere," Mother said. "Somewhere unexpected and fun."

"I could," I said as my mind leapt to the art museum. There was an exhibit of flutes and wind instruments from around the world that I knew Piper would love. We could play music, look at the great pieces of art, and pose with portraits we matched. "I know just the place!"

"Somewhere safe," Mother said, as if she guessed I had mischief in mind. "Somewhere I'd approve of."

I smiled at her with all the beauty of an English rose in the garden. "Somewhere like the park downtown with the big fountain and the ice cream shop?"

"Ice cream?" Piper looked up, brown eyes wide with the joy of hope. His unruly brown hair stuck out at every angle, untamed by any comb.

"Ice cream," I said. "And then another special surprise."

Mother waved goodbye to us and I drove through town, heart racing.

Today was the day.

Today I was going to be where I knew I belonged, in the halls of the masters. Between the greatest pieces of art in the world. Gazing upon a world I knew I would love.

Walking into the museum felt like coming home.

"Oh!" Piper's eyes went wide again and he put a hand over his mouth. "Mommy isn't going to like this."

"Mother doesn't like crowds," I said, repeating her reason. "We're just

going to look around. They have instruments on display."

My brother quivered with youthful anticipation. "Can I play them?"

"Yes."

He darted away, straight for the sign advertising the musical displays. The sound of piping soon filled the air, a romantic melody on a wooden instru-ment, if my ears didn't deceive me.

I floated along after the music, all but dancing through the halls.

This was where I meant to be.

The pipes squeaked as I turned the corner.

Piper stood at the entry to a marble hall with a banner overhead that read HALL OF LOST ART.

Long rows of empty frames hung next to posters of what should have been there. In the center of the hall was a pastoral scene. Oils showed a hazy, dreamy background of pale green hills and soft brown cliffs. A little branch with delicate pink and white flowers balanced out the image of a brown-skinned boy with unruly brown hair sticking out at every angle playing a wooden flute.

Piper.

The print on the poster beside the empty frame was my brother.

He stood in front of it, staring at a painting of himself. "Sophie?"

"Yes, exactly," said a smiling docent quickly. "Sophie Gengembre Anderson, actually. Known for her oil paintings in the pre-Raphaelite style favored by so many Victorian artists."

"Sophie?" Piper turned to me.

I took his hand. "It's a bit... uncanny."

That should have been the end of it.

I should have taken Piper's hand and run home, but I didn't.

We stayed, touring the paintings and posters—until we found one that looked like me.

A young girl in a purple shirt, holding a dove.

A missing painting.

Nothing more.

Nothing more.

Nothing more.

I repeated the words endlessly through each sleepless night.

As I tossed and turned in my uneasy sleep, feeling more and more stretched, more and more consumed with a need to return to the museum.

I tried to stop myself by going to the library. By researching oil paintings. The pre-Raphaelite movement. Everything. Sophie—the artist—I knew every detail of her life. Her beautiful, beautiful work. So lifelike that it glowed.

They said she had been a photographer once, but that she taught herself how to capture people and places on canvas.

How to capture children.

Sleepless weeks crawled by.

Mother said I looked wane. That I needed sun, and a break from studying at the library.

I couldn't tell her. How could I tell her? What could I possibly say?

Then, that morning—oh, that fateful morning…

Piper was waiting for me as the sun rose. He looked exhausted, dark bruises under his brown eyes, his recently cut hair already growing too long and curling in every direction. "Sophie, can we can go back?"

Without thinking, I nodded. "We'll go."

Just to look.

I told myself it was just to look.

We ate breakfast quietly. Solemnly. Trapped in our own thoughts as Mother moved around the house.

She smiled brightly. "Sophie, you're looking well today. Do you have plans?"

"Piper and I were going to go to the park," I said. "Perhaps get some ice cream. Shop for school clothes."

Her mouth tightened into a tight grimace for a moment then her smile returned. "That sounds good. Just remember—"

"No purple and no stripes," I said.

"They give me a headache," Mother said.

"I know."

I washed the bowls before we left. Now, I'm not sure why. Except that it seemed the right thing to do.

The drive was silent, except for Piper's sigh of relief as the museum came into view.

I paid for the tickets and we walked past the instruments, the modern art, the galleries. All that mattered was the hall of lost art.

All that mattered was standing in front of those empty frames.

Piper reached forward, small hand

with those quick, clever fingers pass-
ing the velvet rope. He touched the
frame and his hand went through it.

Color leeched from the frame and
flowed upward.

He looked at me before he faded.
Smiled, just a little.

"Goodbye, Sophie Dove."

"Goodbye, Piper."

When I looked up, it was as if the
canvas had always been there. There
was no poster, or year the painting
went missing. It was simply there, the
perfect painting hanging in the hall
where it didn't belong.

For only a moment I wondered what
people would say.

I wondered if Liza would under-
stand.

Two missing children vanished
from the park. Their car left near the
ice cream shop where it would get a
ticket in an hour when the meter ran
out.

Would they search for us?

Would Mother cry?

Did they search for us before? The nameless mother and father who lost us when we went missing before? When we were captured by oil on canvas?

Did they mourn us?

Or were we forgotten? A pair of pretty paintings and nothing more?

THE MAKING OF
THE ARTIST AS A YOUNG GIRL

What can I say? There was a short story prompt about a little brother crawling into a painting and I grabbed it like a thief and ran with it.

The painting on the cover of this Inklet is a real piece by English artist Sophie Gengembre Anderson and the original belongs to a private collection.

Or does it?

DOWNLOAD YOUR FREE EBOOK

When you buy a print book from Inkprint Press, we like to say THANK YOU by offering you the ebook for free!

Please head to www.inkprintpress.com/inklets/43/ and the use the coupon INK43 to get your copy of this Inklet in epub AND mobi today!
(Coupon will only work once.)

Read more by Liana Brooks!

THE POLAR TERROR

CHAPTER ONE

KADDY LEANED HER HEAD against the pale yellow wall of the hospital room, closed her eyes, and tried not to hear the constant whooshing and beeping of the machines.

The ticky-tick-tick of the heartrate monitor.

The two-minute beep as the IV dropped another controlled dose of pain medications that seemed to do no good.

The whock-whock-whock of the second hand on the clock.

There was no escape.

She couldn't even run outside to the snow and let that peace envelope her. Not while Everett was lying in bed, staring out the window at the flat roof of the parking garage, refusing to talk.

With a sigh, she tried to reach him. Again. "Do you want to watch some TV?"

Everett didn't move.

"We could play with your action figures." She pushed herself out of the uncomfortable chair and walked over to his bed.

Everett let her pull the plush Polar Terror doll out of his listless hand.

She bopped him on the nose with it. "The Polar Terror is coming! He'll walk right out of this storm and—"

Everett rolled to the side, crossing his tiny arms as best he could. His bottom lip quavered with anger and pain.

"I'm sorry." Kaddy put the doll back next to him. "We're going to find a way through this, Ev. I promise. And then we'll sew you the Polar Terror costume you wanted."

"There is no Polar Terror," Everett whispered, his first words all day. "Nobody comes to rescue you."

She rubbed his shoulder gently. "I know, bud. That's why you have me. You and me, we can handle anything."

"Not this," he whispered. "Not cancer."

Tears choked her. "We will," she whispered just as a softly. "We'll find a way to make it all right."

Everett squeezed his eyes shut.

Kaddy slumped back. Even if—and it was a really big if—the hospital pulled off a miracle and Everett got better, she wasn't going back to a job.

Her firm had been very patient, let her take a leave of absence, but her boss was retiring and the incoming boss hadn't liked her.

He'd questioned her education, her field time, her work ethic...

And while the guy couldn't come out and say it, his tone all but screamed SINGLE MOMS NEED NOT APPLY.

She shook her head. Being a single mom hadn't been her choice. She wasn't even dating when Everett was born.

But then there'd been a car accident a semester before graduation. Her sister and brother-in-law were killed on impact.

The idea of being a working, single parent was terrifying, but letting Everett bounce between foster families wasn't an option either.

Squeezing the guard rail of his hospital bed, she stood up. One way or another, she'd make a good life for him. That's what moms did.

There was a tentative knock at the door, like the person on the other side was hoping they wouldn't get an answer, but knew they would.

Rolling her eyes, Kaddy cracked it open for the inevitable nurse.

Andrea, the ever-perky Dream Coordinator for Merriton Pediatric Hospital, looked at her with the world's fakest smile, wide, frightened blue eyes, and damp blonde hair that looked like she'd gone outside without her usual hat.

"Yessssss?" Kaddy dragged the word out.

Andrea squeezed through the tiny crack in the doorway and slammed the door shut. "Okay. Hi, Kaddy! Everett! It is so good to see you two!" The words were rushed, panicked, and had the forced joviality of true terror.

But this was the Yukon in mid-winter, not some American city where a bomber was going to hold them hostage. "Is... is everything okay?" Kaddy asked.

The only thing that would scare Andrea was a really bad diagnosis. Kaddy's stomach flipped as tears welled. She couldn't handle that.

"Just dandy!" Andrea's voice squeaked. "Actually." She faked a laugh. "Funny story. Everett has a visitor. And, I know he's been so tuckered out, the poor thing, so I was thinking we should reschedule. Don't you? That's great!" she rushed on, not letting Kaddy answer. "I'll cancel. He can come back some other time."

Not bad news then.

Everett rolled over in his bed, forehead wrinkled in confusion.

"Who came?" Kaddy asked. The hospital attracted an eclectic group of visitors. Usually hockey stars, medical students, and politicians on goodwill tours. But Andrea welcomed them all with open arms. "It isn't the Maple Leafs again, is it?" No one this far north loved the Maple Leafs.

Andrea's head shook so hard Kaddy worried the woman was going to give herself a concussion.

"Okay…"

Kaddy glanced over at Everett who was showing the first interest in anything since his chemo treatment two days earlier. "Is there a reason you don't want this person to see Everett?" She licked her lips and mouthed, *Is it child services?*

"Worse," Andrea whispered hoarsely. She leaned forward and murmured a name in Kaddy's ear.

Kaddy's eyebrows went up in surprise. "Like... for real? You—" She stopped herself just in time and leaned forward. "You found a cosplayer to play the Polar Terror?"

She couldn't keep the excitement out of her whisper. Everett was going to be over the moon.

"No." Andrea shook her head and glanced over her shoulder. The color drained from her face. "He's... he's not fake."

"Who isn't fake?" Everett demanded from the bed.

"Just say no." Andrea grabbed Kaddy's elbow. "Please?"

Kaddy shook the other woman off and looked at the door.

There was a thin layer of frost on the door. A suspiciously thin layer. Like someone was intentionally cooling the door for a grand entrance.

She narrowed her eyes. Would the Dream Coordinator come in here acting terrified just to sell the idea of a super villain at the hospital? Yes. Yes she would. It was *exactly* the sort of thing a perky, cheerful-before-coffee, former cheer-leader would do.

Kaddy crossed her arms and sighed dramatically. "I don't know, Andrea. Ev's had a really rough week. I don't think he should have visitors. Not even the Polar Terror."

The heartrate monitor screamed in excitement as Everett sat up like he was attached to a spring. "The Polar Terror?"

With a burst of cold air, the door fell inward. Ice crystals glittered as icicles formed on the ceiling.

That was some impressive special effects budget.

A man in the Polar Terror's costume stepped in, towering over even Kaddy, who hadn't been called short since she turned thirteen and shot up. The muskrat parka, a rabbit fur hat, a strip of seal skin, a fur pouch, beadwork on his boots... and of course the very modern black balaclava with the Under Armor logo.

The Polar Terror had come to Merriton.

Keep reading! Head to www.lianabrooks.com/ polar-terror/
to buy your copy now!

ABOUT THE AUTHOR

LIANA BROOKS earned her first and only B in 2nd grade art class because she failed to accurately draw leaves laying on a page. She's never been particularly good at drawing, but she appreciates the skill in others, even if she suspects there is some sort of magic involved.

Brooks is known for her space operas, including the *Fleet of Malik,* a series of connected sci-fi romances about re-building after a decades long war; and the enemies-to-lovers super-hero series, *Heroes and Villains*.

You can find out more about Liana at her website, www.lianabrooks.com.

INKLETS

Collect them all! Released on the 1st and 15th of each month.

INKLET #031
Welcome to Dark Dale
LIANA BROOKS

INKLET #032
When War Came to Town
A Powers Story
AMY LAURENS

INKLET #033
Not Fantasy
AMY LAURENS

INKLET #034
Courting the Winter Prince
LIANA BROOKS

INKLET #035
At the Home of the Winter King
A Storm Foxes Story
AMY LAURENS

INKLET #036
With This Ring
AMY LAURENS

INKLET #037
Venus &
Seven Reasons I Said No
LIANA BROOKS

INKLET #038
OATH KEEPER
AMY LAURENS

INKLET #039
FORGET
A Powers Story
AMY LAURENS

INKLET #040
NOT QUITE
Cinderella
LIANA BROOKS

INKLET #041
ONE BAD MAN
AMY LAURENS

DOUBLE ISSUE
INKLET #042
The Claustrophobia
Of Loneliness &
Adam, Be A Star
AMY LAURENS

INKLET #043
The Artist
as a Young Girl
LIANA BROOKS

INKLET #044
Confessions
AMY LAURENS

INKLET #045
But For Snow
A Kaditeos Story
AMY LAURENS

INKLET #046
The Boy
Named NO
LIANA BROOKS

INKLET #047
Anamata
AMY LAURENS

INKLET #048
A Wolf FOR
Christmas
AMY LAURENS

www.ingramcontent.com/pod-product-compliance
Lightning Source LLC
Chambersburg PA
CBHW051303190726
48286CB00004B/1236